Nick Fury, director of S.H.I.E.L.D., is a busy man. After months of searching for Captain America in the Arctic, coddling Tony Stark and monitoring the unstable Bruce Banner, Fury's been reassigned. The World Security Council has charged him instead with unlocking the mysteries of the Tesseract, a mysterious alien cube containing seemingly limitless energy. But Fury has other plans...

JIM ZUB SCRIPT

WOO BIN CHOI WITH **JAE SUNG LEE** ART

MIN JU LEE INKS

JAE WOONG LEE, HEE YE CHO & IN YOUNG LEE COLORS

VC's CORY PETIT LETTERS

WOO BIN CHOI WITH **JAE SUNG LEE, MIN JU LEE, JAE WOONG LEE & HEE YE CHO** COVER ART

Adapted from *MARVEL'S AVENGERS PRELUDE: FURY'S BIG WEEK #1-4.*
Adaptations written by SI YEON PARK and translated by JI EUN PARK

AVENGERS created by STAN LEE and JACK KIRBY

Original comics written by CHRIS YOST and ERIC PEARSON; and illustrated by LUKE ROSS, DANIEL HDR, AGUSTIN PADILLA, DON HO, WELLINTON ALVES, RICK KETCHAM, MARK PENNINGTON and CHRIS SOTOMAYOR

Editor SARAH BRUNSTAD
Manager, Licensed Publishing JEFF REINGOLD
VP Brand Management & Development, Asia C.B. CEBULSKI
VP Production & Special Projects JEFF YOUNGQUIST
SVP Print, Sales & Marketing DAVID GABRIEL
Associate Manager, Digital Assets JOE HOCHSTEIN
Associate Managing Editor KATERI WOODY
Assistant Editor CAITLIN O'CONNELL
Senior Editor, Special Projects JENNIFER GRÜNWALD
Editor, Special Projects MARK D. BEAZLEY
Book Designer: ADAM DEL RE

Editor In Chief AXEL ALONSO
Chief Creative Officer JOE QUESADA
President DAN BUCKLEY
Executive Producer ALAN FINE

EXTRAORDINARY ALLIES

PHIL COULSON

WAR MACHINE

JANE FOSTER

AVENGERS MOST WANTED

WHIPLASH

LOKI

DESTROYER

ABOMINATION

SAMUEL STERNS

ABDOPUBLISHING.COM

Reinforced library bound edition published in 2018 by Spotlight, a division of ABDO, PO Box 398166, Minneapolis, Minnesota 55439.
Spotlight produces high-quality reinforced library bound editions for schools and libraries. Published by agreement with Marvel Characters, Inc.
Printed in the United States of America, North Mankato, Minnesota.
092017 012018

PUBLISHER'S CATALOGING-IN-PUBLICATION DATA

Names: Zub, Jim, author. | Choi, Woo Bin; Lee, Jae Sung; Lee, Min Ju; Lee, Jae Woong; Cho, Hee Ye; Lee, In Young, illustrators.
Title: Assembling the Avengers / writer: Jim Zub ; art: Woo Bin Choi; Jae Sung Lee; Min Ju Lee; Jae Woong Lee; Hee Ye Cho; In Young Lee.
Description: Minneapolis, MN : Spotlight, 2018 | Series: Avengers K Set 3
Summary: With a changing world full of threats bigger than he could imagine, S.H.I.E.L.D. director Nick Fury struggles to follow orders from the World Security Council. He calls upon Agent Coulson, Hawkeye, and Black Widow for aid to search for the missing Captain America, help Tony Stark fix his failing arc reactor in his chest, stop the Hulk from going on a rampage, and unearth an alien object, followed shortly by its electrifying owner.
Identifiers: LCCN 2017941923 | ISBN 9781532141478 (v.1 ; lib. bdg.) | ISBN 9781532141485 (v.2 ; lib. bdg.) | ISBN 9781532141492 (v.3 ; lib. bdg.) | ISBN 9781532141508 (v.4 ; lib. bdg.) | ISBN 9781532141515 (v.5 ; lib. bdg.) | ISBN 9781532141522 (v.6 ; lib. bdg.) | ISBN 9781532141539 (v.7 ; lib.bdg.)
Subjects: LCSH: Avengers (ficitious character)--Juvenile fiction. | Super heroes--Juvenile fiction. | Graphic Novels--Juvenile fiction. | Media Tie-in--Juvenile fiction.
Classification: DDC 741.5--dc23
LC record available at http://lccn.loc.gov/2017941923

A Division of ABDO
abdopublishing.com

"IRON MAN:
OUT OF CONTROL"
PART 1

ONE DAY LATER.
NEW YORK CITY IS UNDER ATTACK FROM AN UNKNOWN ASSAILANT...
THIS BATTLE HAS ALREADY CAUSED UNTOLD AMOUNTS OF PROPERTY DAMAGE...
IRON MAN APPEARS TO BE INVOLVED...
WHAT A MESS...
I NEVER SHOULD'VE ANSWERED THAT PHONE CALL...

ONE WEEK EARLIER.

RIIING

RIIING
RIIING

FURY HERE.

SIR, IN 72 HOURS TONY STARK WILL BE DEAD.
WHAT?!

DIRECTOR FURY!
IT'S BEEN CHAOS HERE!
THE PHONES HAVE BEEN RINGING OFF THE HOOK.

SENATOR STERN WANTS TO DISCUSS ACQUIRING THE IRON MAN TECHNOLOGY.

DELAY HIM FOR NOW. TELL HIM I'M DEALING WITH NATIONAL SECURITY ISSUES.

I NEED YOUR SIGNATURE FOR THE BUDGET REDISTRIBUTION.

AGENT SITWELL REPORTS THAT BANNER JUST CLEARED CUSTOMS.

TELL SITWELL TO STAY ON HIM.
YES, SIR.

SIR, GENERAL ROSS IS ASKING FOR--
TELL HIM "NO."

DIRECTOR FURY...
WHAT IS IT, AGENT COULSON?

THERE'S SOMETHING YOU NEED TO SEE.

NOT SURE IF YOU NOTICED, BUT I'M A LITTLE BUSY RIGHT NOW...
MY TEAM HAS PICKED UP AN ATMOSPHERIC DISTURBANCE ABOVE NEW MEXICO.

SINCE WHEN DID S.H.I.E.L.D. BECOME THE WEATHER CHANNEL?
I WOULDN'T BRING IT UP IF IT WASN'T IMPORTANT.

THE ELECTROMAGNETIC SIGNATURES ARE OFF THE CHARTS.

DO YOU HAVE AN EXPLANATION FOR IT? ANY THEORIES?

NOTHING YET.

GET BACK TO ME WHEN YOU DO. UNTIL THEN, I'VE GOT MORE IMPORTANT THINGS TO DEAL WITH.

ALL RIGHT PEOPLE, WHO'S GOT ANSWERS FOR ME?

DIRECTOR FURY!
GOOD TIMING, SIR!

THANKS FOR RESPONDING SO QUICKLY TO MY CALL. TAKE A LOOK HERE.

WE DID EXTENSIVE ANALYSIS ON TONY STARK'S BLOOD SAMPLE.

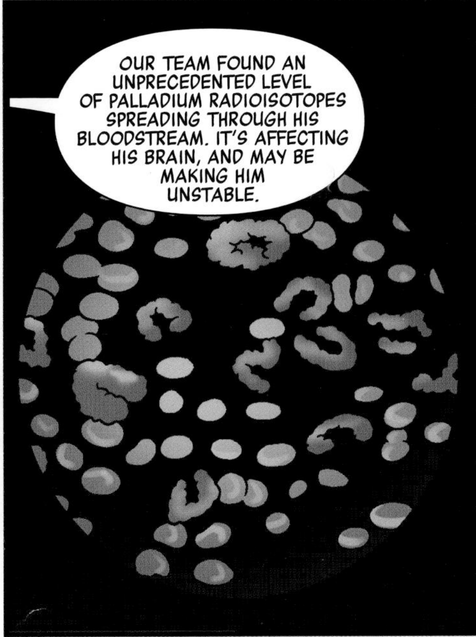
OUR TEAM FOUND AN UNPRECEDENTED LEVEL OF PALLADIUM RADIOISOTOPES SPREADING THROUGH HIS BLOODSTREAM. IT'S AFFECTING HIS BRAIN, AND MAY BE MAKING HIM UNSTABLE.

WE BELIEVE IT'S RELATED TO THE ARC REACTOR EMBEDDED IN HIS CHEST. PALLADIUM IS A TRICKY ELEMENT.
SO HE'LL BE DEAD WITHIN 72 HOURS?

YES, SIR.

WELL, WHAT'S THE NEXT STEP?

IS THERE A CURE?

NOTHING SAFE.

WHAT'S THAT SUPPOSED TO MEAN?

I HAVEN'T GOT TIME TO PLAY GAMES.
I UNDERSTAND, IT'S JUST THAT THIS PROCEDURE IS UNTESTED AND QUITE DANGEROUS.

SHOW ME.
LITHIUM DIOXIDE. IT'S NOT A CURE, BUT IT MIGHT BUY HIM MORE TIME.

CAN'T YOU MAKE IT STRONGER? PERMANENT?

THERE'S NOTHING ON EARTH THAT CAN COUNTER THIS LEVEL OF PALLADIUM BUILDUP.

AND YOU SHOULD ALSO KNOW...

THERE'S A SLIM CHANCE THE INJECTION WILL KILL HIM INSTANTLY.

WHAT?! WHY DIDN'T YOU START WITH THAT?!

BZZZT

NICK, IT'S NATASHA. STARK'S LOSING CONTROL.

HOW BAD IS IT?

PRETTY BAD.

AHHHH!
TONY AND HIS PAL JAMES RHODES ARE TRASHING STARK'S MANSION.
WHACK

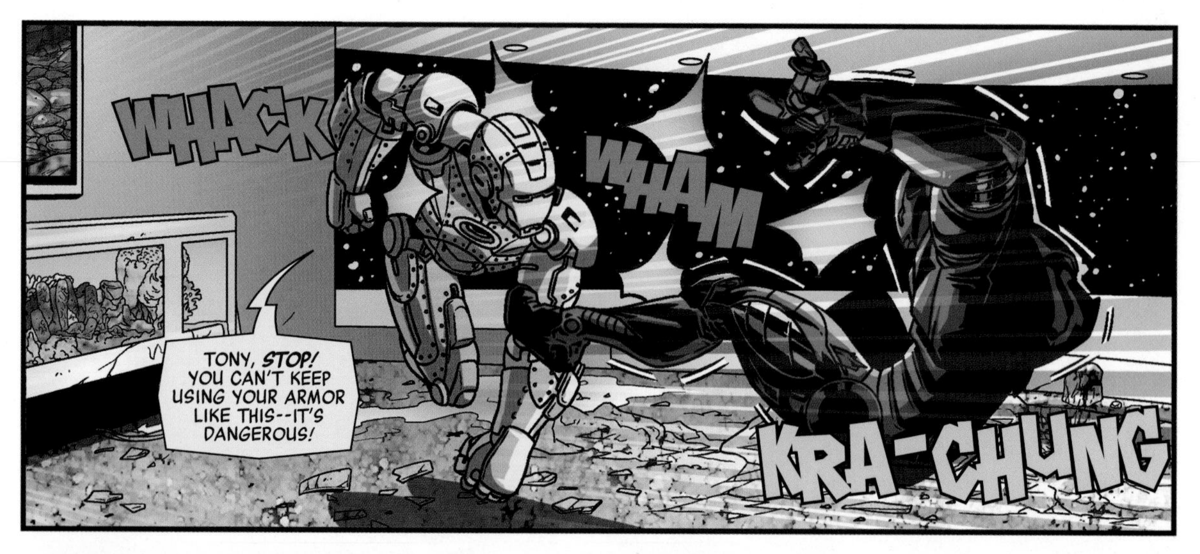
WHACK
WHAM
TONY, **STOP!** YOU CAN'T KEEP USING YOUR ARMOR LIKE THIS--IT'S DANGEROUS!
KRA-CHUNG

I TOLD YOU, RHODEY...
WHOOSH

THAK

...LEAVE ME **ALONE!**

KRANG

KA-BLAM

STAY PUT, AND DON'T BLOW YOUR COVER. I'M ON MY WAY.

DON'T BOTHER. THEY JUST LEFT.

HOLD TIGHT. I'LL GET BACK TO YOU.

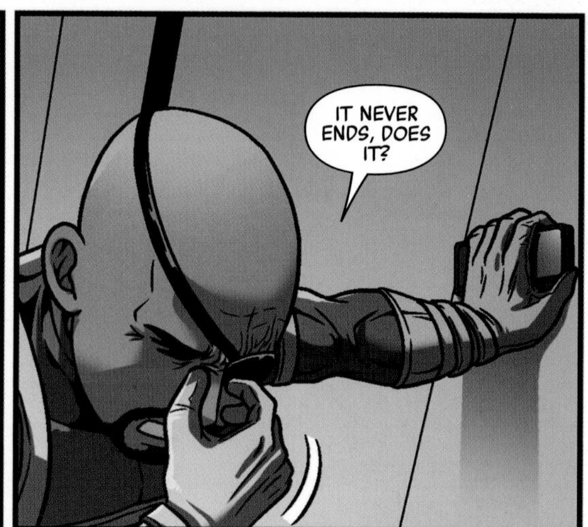
IT NEVER ENDS, DOES IT?

SIR, IF YOU'D JUST LOOK AT THESE GLACIER READINGS, YOU'D SEE...

IT'LL HAVE TO WAIT, COULSON.
GET ME A LINE TO THE WORLD SECURITY COUNCIL. NOW!

BZZZT

I APOLOGIZE, DIRECTOR. YOU WILL NEED TO WAIT A FEW MORE MINUTES.

SIR, WE'VE LOCATED TONY STARK.
WHERE?

STAY HIDDEN. WHEN YOU SEE AN OPENING...

...STICK HIM IN THE NECK WITH *THIS.*

YES, SIR.

47 MILES OUTSIDE ROSWELL, NEW MEXICO.
DARCY, COME LOOK AT THIS! THESE READINGS ARE OFF THE CHARTS!

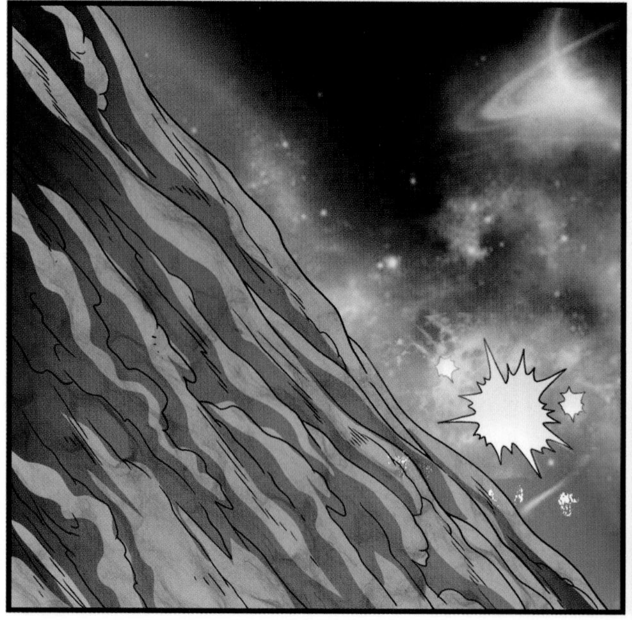

TONY STARK'S MANSION. MALIBU, CALIFORNIA.

STARK SURE KNOWS HOW TO THROW A PARTY.
SIR, THERE'S BEEN ANOTHER FLARE UP.

ENLARGE SCREEN SEVEN.

THAT'S THE THIRD FLARE TODAY.
IT'S WITHIN EARTH'S ATMOSPHERE, SIR.

EACH ONE IS THE SAME. EACH INCIDENT HAS RESULTED IN SOME GRAVITATIONAL LENSING.

IT'S ALMOST AS THOUGH THERE'S SOMETHING TRYING TO PUSH THROUGH THE SPACE-TIME CONTINUUM.
AGREED.
GRAVITATIONAL LENSING: A PHENOMENON BY WHICH LIGHT TRAVELING THROUGH THE GRAVITATIONAL FIELD OF A MASSIVE OBJECT--LIKE A BLACK HOLE--BENDS AROUND THAT OBJECT, CAUSING IT TO APPEAR IN A DIFFERENT SHAPE. THAT'S WHY GALAXIES SOMETIMES LOOK LIKE ARCS OR RINGS!

BUT THAT'S IMPOSSIBLE, RIGHT?
I'VE LEARNED NOT TO USE THAT WORD ANYMORE.

HEY, COULSON. WHO GAVE YOU PERMISSION TO DIG THROUGH MY STUFF?

DIRECTOR FURY. HE THOUGHT YOU COULD USE A CLEANUP CREW AFTER WHAT HAPPENED.

IS THAT SO? WELL, MAKE YOURSELF AT HOME.

THANK YOU, I WILL.

AGENT COULSON VOICE-PRINT VERIFIED. TRANSFERRING TO DIRECTOR FURY...

SIR, THE SITUATION IN NEW MEXICO LOOKS SERIOUS. I NEED A FACE-TO-FACE.

TO BE CONTINUED!